Laura Langston & Lindsey Gardiner

Mile-High Apple Pie

RED FOX

This book belongs to

. . . .

For Julia Eisler, who shares her soul so generously – Laura

For my mum and Fran (and many misplaced memories!) – Lin

MILE-HIGH APPLE PIE
A RED FOX BOOK : 978 0 099 44388 9
(from January 2007)
0 099 44388 0

First published in Great Britain by The Bodley Head,
an imprint of Random House Children's Books

The Bodley Head edition published 2004
Red Fox edition published 2005

3 5 7 9 10 8 6 4 2

Text copyright © Laura Langston, 2004
Illustrations copyright © Lindsey Gardiner, 2004

The right of Laura Langston and Lindsey Gardiner to be identified as the
author and illustrator of this work has been asserted in accordance
with the Copyright, Designs and Patents Act 1988.

Visit Laura Langston's website at www.lauralansgton.com

Red Fox Books are published by Random House Children's Books,
61–63 Uxbridge Road, London W5 5SA,
a division of The Random House Group Ltd,
London Sydney Auckland Johannesburg
and agencies throughout the world

THE RANDOM HOUSE GROUP Limited Reg. No. 954009
www.kidsatrandomhouse.co.uk

A CIP catalogue record for this book is available from the British Library.

Printed in Singapore

My grandma lives with us now because she can't remember. She is not the wrinkled kind; she's the special kind instead. She wears trainers with yellow laces and she laughs very loud. Once she had a houseboat and an art gallery by the sea. Then, she played the piano and made mile-high apple pie.

Now, she sits in her special chair and rocks quick, quick, quick.

Dad says that one day Grandma's remembering will go away for ever.

She will forget everything, even our names. He is wrong.

Grandma still reads me stories,

only now I help her with the words.

We still go outside to play, and Grandma still talks to the birds.

We **giggle** and **laugh** and **sing** special songs together.

When Grandma gets mixed up, I tell her it's time for a nap. I keep her company while she rests.

Some days, Grandma jumps when her very own cat lands on her lap.
"And **who** are **you**?" she asks.

"That's Princess Pepper," I say. "She loves you very much."
I feed the cat and comb the tangles out of her fur.

She keeps my
grandma warm.

After school, I practise the piano. Sometimes Grandma
nods her head and doesn't say anything at all.
Other times she tells me how well *I* have done.

"Excellent, Margaret,"

she says. "Chopin
would be proud."

I give her a hug. I was playing Bach
but Grandma can't remember.

Grandma still plants sweet peas
in spring.

"They are the only flower worth growing,"
she says, "because they smell so wonderful."

The flowers grow **tall** and **pretty**. I cut a huge handful and bring them inside. I put them under Grandma's nose. "Smell."

"**Lovely**," she says. "Roses are my favourite flower."

She rocks her chair quick, quick, quick.

Princess Pepper jumps down.

"It's OK," Mum whispers when she sees me frown. "She loves them anyway."

In the autumn,
Grandma helps me
pick apples
to make pie.

"I like those pears," she says. "I must pick them for my purse and put them in preserves."

I giggle.
"They are apples, Grandma.
They are for our pie,
remember?"

"No," she says with a frown.
"That's OK," I say. "I'll
remember for you."

Dad bakes her favourite
mile-high apple pie now,
and Grandma helps.
"Peel them this way."
She shows me how to take
the skin from the apple.
When I cut away the bruise,
Grandma stops me.

"The bruise is the best," she says.
"All the sweetness in the apple rushes to the soft, brown bit."
Dad laughs but Grandma insists.
"I remember," she says.
"A fruit man told me once."

We keep the bruised bits in our mile-high apple pie. Because Grandma remembered.

Grandma likes to take Princess Pepper
for a walk. Sometimes I go with them.
Grandma remembers
lots of things –
like steam trains
and milk carts
and rationing.

But she can't remember the way home. Yesterday, she went into a neighbour's house **by mistake.**

Grandma's remembering is getting worse.

One day after school, Grandma is in her chair rocking quick, quick, quick.

She smiles at me when I come close.

"And Who are you, my dear?"

At first I think she's teasing. But then
I see that look on her face and I know.

My head
goes all
whooshy;
my eyes
start to
sting.

Grandma
can't
remember
who
I am.
I go to my room without
giving her a hug.

"Grandma's brain is all **mixed** up,"
Mum says as she rubs my back.
"But she still loves you,
even if she can't remember your name."

Now, I let Mum take Grandma for walks.
I practise the piano when she's not around.

Sometimes I wish I could
crawl into Grandma's lap
like Princess Pepper.
And other times I wish
Grandma didn't live
here any more.

One day, Grandma leaves for a week.
"We need a break," Dad says.
Princess Pepper stays behind. She prowls
    and meows and can't find a place to settle.
I have three friends over at once
    and we make lots of noise.

Mum makes
spicy chips and
pepperoni pizza, the
things Grandma hates.

But no one sits in
the special chair
and rocks

quick,
quick,
quick.

Grandma comes back on a sunny afternoon.
She sits in her chair and pats
Princess Pepper on the head.

I watch her and wonder.

Will she
know me
today?

She pulls me close.
"**Hello, my dear,**" she says.
"Do you know who I am?" I ask.
Grandma's eyes look confused.
Finally, she laughs.
"You are my sweetness. The one who
brings me flowers and plays the piano.
You are my apple-cheeked bruise girl."

At first, I
don't understand.
But then
I smile.

I am like the
sweet bits in Grandma's
mile-high apple pie.
Her favourite food.

I push Princess Pepper
over and crawl into
Grandma's lap.

"I am
Margaret,"
I say.

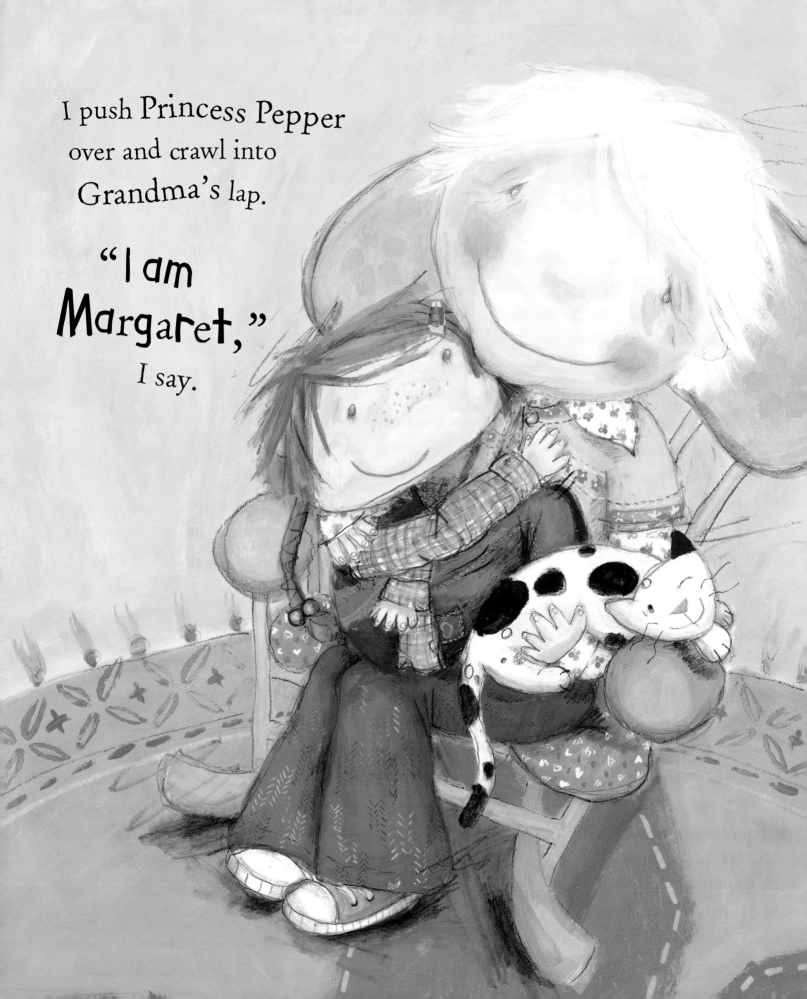

"I am your remembering."

MILE-HIGH APPLE PIE

10 Granny Smith apples
180 g/6 oz white sugar
60 g/3 oz plain flour
5 ml/1 tsp ground nutmeg
15 ml/1 tbsp ground cinnamon
a pinch ground cloves
a pinch of salt
30 g/1 oz butter
Prepared pastry for a
double crust pie
1 egg beaten with
1 tbsp water

Preheat the oven to 190°C (gas mark 5).
Grease a large pie dish.
Roll out the pastry on a lightly floured surface.
Line the pie dish with the pastry, keeping half for the top crust.

Ask an adult to help core, peel and slice the apples.
Mix the sugar, flour, cinnamon, nutmeg, cloves, salt and butter.
Add the apples, mix well, and pour mixture into the pastry dish.
Dot with butter. Cover with top crust, sealing carefully. Make slits.

Beat the egg and water. Brush over the top of the pastry.

Ask an adult to help with the oven.

Cover the dish with kitchen foil and bake for 25–30 minutes.
Remove the foil and bake another 25–30 minutes
or until crust is nicely browned.
Take your MILE-HIGH APPLE PIE out of the oven.

If you liked this story, why not try:

Granpa

BY JOHN BURNINGHAM

Katie Morag and the Two Grandmothers

BY MAIRI HEDDERWICK

In a Little While

BY CHARLOTTE HUDSON AND MARY McQUILLAN

Elmer and Grandpa Eldo

BY DAVID McKEE